THE BOY
PALE I

A STORY OF THE INDUS VALLEY

by Helen Cannam
Illustrated by Robin Lawrie

ANGLIA *a* BOOKS
young

First published in 2003
by Anglia Young Books

Anglia Young Books is an imprint of
Mill Publishing Ltd
PO Box 120
Bangor
County Down BT19 7BX

Illustrations by Robin Lawrie
Design by Angela Ashton

British Library Cataloguing-in-Publication Data

A catalogue record for this book is available from the British Library

ISBN 1 871173 92 2

Printed in Great Britain by Ashford Colour Press, Gosport, Hampshire

For Jonah, with love

The Ancient Indus Valley Civilisation

WHERE IT WAS

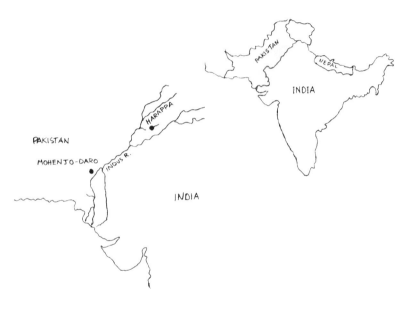

AUTHOR'S NOTE

The cities of the Indus Valley civilisation were built and lived in around four thousand years ago. The houses the people lived in have been found, as well as some of the goods they made, such as pottery, jewellery, toys, pieces of cloth, and the seals they used for trading.

Archaeologists know that the Indus Valley people lived by trade, exchanging goods they made for goods they wanted from other places. They know, too, that they used the annual floods of the River Indus and its tributaries to help them grow enough food for all the people in the cities. The food was probably stored in huge granaries to be given out to the people as they needed it.

But no one is quite sure what the Indus Valley people looked like, what language they spoke, what religion they believed in, or who ruled them and how. There are lots of different ideas about these things. In writing this story, I've had to decide some things for myself, so I could be quite wrong about them! Perhaps one day the archaeologists will find out all the things we don't yet know.

CHAPTER ONE

Atek hammered at the rock with a stone. His hands were sore. Small pieces of rock flew up and hit his face or his arms. He ached all over. It took a long time to crush the rock into small pieces, to get at the silver ore inside it. When it was ready, the ore would be heated in a very hot fire until it melted. Then it would be poured into a mould to cool into blocks of silver called ingots.

Usually, Atek had other people to help him, but today he was working alone. Men kept bringing him more rock to crush, just got out of the ground from the pit in the woods.

An evil-smelling, choking smoke blew his way from the place where his uncle Janaki was smelting the ore to get out the silver. Further off, he could hear the voices of his cousins, shouting and laughing. They were gathering wood for the fire, a nice, easy job, even though they were older than Atek and stronger.

Soon, Atek knew, his uncle would come and see how he was getting on. 'I need that ore today, White Eyes,' he would say. 'Not the day after tomorrow.' And he would hit Atek round the head before he went back to the fierce, hot fire on the hilltop.

Three men came down the hill, passing close to Atek. He bent his head, waiting for one of them to laugh at him or kick him. It wasn't just his uncle who called him 'White Eyes' and treated him like dirt. They all did. Atek had never seen what his eyes looked like, but he imagined them, blank and white and horrible – the sort of eyes that frightened people and made them think he was some sort of monster.

To his relief the men were so busy talking they went past without even looking at him. They were talking about the traders who had come to the village yesterday, from the cities by the Great River. They came every few months, bringing all kinds of goods for the village, cloth and jewellery and spices and other things people wanted, or so the men were saying. Atek had seen the packages the traders had brought when the cart first rolled into the village – they had been wrapped in sacking and marked with seals, with pictures on them and strange lines. The traders had come for silver. The people in the cities of the Great River had no silver of their own, so they sent the things they made to the village to exchange for a load of silver. Once the ingots were loaded on the cart, the traders would set out again on their long journey home. 'I wish I could go away with them,' Atek thought, 'like my father did.'

'White Eyes!' His uncle was shouting for him. Atek dropped the stone hammer and ran up the hill. He stood before his uncle, gasping for breath, waiting to hear what he had done wrong.

'Get down to the house and fetch me some food,' Janaki said. 'I've no time to stop work today.'

He didn't seem to have time, either, for hitting Atek, because he simply turned his back on the boy.

Relieved, Atek ran off at once, down the hill, along the dusty track between the trees, to the hut – the largest in the village – where his uncle's family lived.

His aunt, Kamala, was sitting outside, spinning wool from the village goats. She smiled as he came up to her. She was the only person who ever treated him with kindness, though most of the time it was a secret kindness. She was almost as afraid of Janaki as Atek was. 'What's this? Has your uncle given you some time off?'

Atek knew she was teasing. Janaki never gave anyone any time off, not even his own sons. 'He sent me for some food.'

Kamala put down her spindle and led the way into the hut. She wrapped up two lentil cakes, made that morning, and a handful of dates. Atek watched her, with his mind on other things. 'Aunt, do you think my father will ever come back?' he asked suddenly.

Kamala stopped what she was doing and gazed at him. 'Oh, Atek, he went away long, long years ago, when you were just a baby. He would have come back by now, if he was going to.' She ran her

hand up and down his arm. 'Why do you ask about him all of a sudden?'

'I just wondered, that's all. Why did he go away?'

'He wanted to see the cities by the Great River. So he went off with some traders. He never came back. Nor did the men who went with him – though they weren't villagers, so that wasn't so strange.'

'What do you think happened?'

'I don't know, but I think he must be dead by now. He promised to come back, and he loved you and your mother very much. He wouldn't have stayed away from choice.' She looked very sad, even now. Atek knew she had been fond of her brother, his father. 'Do you remember him at all?' she asked.

Atek shook his head. 'I can hardly even remember my mother now,' he admitted. She had died a few years after his father left, of a fever that had killed many people in the village. Atek remembered her mostly as a warm, happy feeling somewhere inside him, and then a great sadness. 'What was my father like?'

'You're very like him,' said his aunt. 'Romesh was a fine-looking man. You have his eyes.'

'White eyes?' Atek shuddered. How could his aunt call him fine-looking, if he had white eyes?

Kamala smiled. Atek could see she was remembering the brother who had gone away all those years ago. 'Your eyes aren't white,' she said. 'I know that's what they call you, but it's not true. They're more the colour of –' She stopped and thought hard for a moment. 'The ore, when it comes out of the ground. Even the silver. But not so cold or so hard. Sometimes the sky's that colour.'

Atek found it hard to imagine the colour she was describing. Kamala's eyes were brown, like everyone else's in the village. He'd always wished his were the same, but now he was cheered to think he was like his father. If only his father had still been here, then everything would have been different! 'If my eyes aren't so bad, why does everyone laugh at me for them?' he wondered now.

'Some people just don't like anything different,' said his aunt. 'It frightens them. But they don't like to admit they're frightened, so they call it unlucky or bad. Some of them even say it means you have magic powers.'

'I wish I had,' said Atek. 'Then I could make them leave me alone.'

Kamala hugged him. 'Always remember, your father was a good man – kind to his friends and to those in need, wise and just to everyone. Try to be like him.' Then she straightened up. 'Now, you'd better take this food to your uncle, quickly, or you'll be in trouble.'

CHAPTER TWO

On his way back up the hill, Atek passed the traders. They were sitting in the shade under the trees, with food spread on the ground beside them, resting before the long journey that would begin in a few days, when the silver would be ready to be packed on their bullock cart. 'I wish I could go with them,' Atek thought. Then an idea struck him. 'Perhaps Kamala's wrong. Perhaps my father's still alive. If I went with them, I might find him.'

He told himself it was silly to think like that. Kamala was right. His father must be dead. On the other hand, he thought, as the stink of the smoke reached him, and he heard his uncle's voice, shouting at someone, would it matter even if he didn't find his father? He couldn't be worse off, away from here, away from all these people who treated him so badly.

But the traders would never agree to take him away with them, not without his uncle's permission, and he was quite sure his uncle would refuse to let him go. He was too useful as a kind of slave, someone who would do all the nasty jobs, someone who could be kicked when anyone felt cross about anything at all.

His cousins Kav and Shanki had been wrestling together somewhere in the wood. They rolled down the slope from the trees onto the path in front of him. He got ready to run, but he was too late. They had seen him.

Kav pulled at the parcel of food. 'What's this then, White Eyes?' He snatched it and threw it to his brother. Lentil cakes and dates spilled onto the ground.

'Don't! That's for your father!'

Shanki tripped him up and sent him sprawling.

'Then he's going to be very angry with you, isn't he? You should be more careful, you useless lump of dirt!'

By the time Atek was on his feet again, his cousins had crushed the food under their feet. There was no hope that he could pick it up and pretend nothing had happened to it. Nor, he knew, was there any hope that he could shift the blame onto them. He would have to go back for some more food.

Fortunately, his aunt had just started doing some more cooking, so there were fresh cakes for him to take. He ran all the way back up the hill.

As he had expected, Janaki was angry that he had taken so long. He put the food in a safe place and then beat Atek, before sending him back to his work breaking up the rocks.

When it grew too dark to see what he was doing, Atek was allowed to stop work. By the time he got back to the hut, everyone else was there, sitting round the fire eating supper. His aunt slipped him some food, which he ate outside. Then, when they all went to bed, he curled up in a corner near the door, wrapped in his rough cloak. As he lay down, he reached a hand out and felt for the thing he had hidden under a stone in the darkest place, where he hoped no one would find it. It was made of wood, a tiny whistle, shaped like a bird. His father had made it for him, his baby son, before he left on that last journey. It was the only thing Atek owned, apart from his clothes. Every night he would fall asleep with his fingers closed around it.

But tonight was different. As he drifted off to sleep, he thought of the idea that had come to him that afternoon. He made a decision: 'I shall run away. I shall go with the traders, somehow. And if my father's still alive, I shall find him.'

During the next few days he made his plans. Whenever he could, he watched the traders, seeing where they left their belongings, how they loaded the bullock cart, piece by piece, with the articles they were taking with them – all but the silver, which would go on at the last moment. He saw that when they were eating their meals, they usually sat away from the cart, with their backs to it. They had a small dog with them, which followed them everywhere and which they fed with titbits from their own food.

At last the silver was ready. That morning, Atek was, as usual, supposed to be breaking up the rocks. But his uncle was busy supervising the loading of the cart and making the final arrangements with the traders, so he did not notice that Atek had left his place and was hiding in the trees watching what was going on. As he watched, Atek clutched the bird whistle, to remind himself why he was going to do such a risky thing.

The silver was loaded, wrapped in sacking, and goat skins that would be exchanged along with the silver. 'We'll have a last drink together before you go,' Janaki said. He was being pleasant to the men, wanting them to do some good trading for him. They all went off towards his hut, the dog following them.

Atek crept out of the trees and hurried over to the cart. The two bullocks, still waiting to be hitched up to the cart, watched him with gentle eyes. No one else was watching. He climbed onto the back of the

cart and slid under the skins that covered the load, right in the middle between two parcels of silver. It was not very comfortable. Even well wrapped up, the silver was hard and knobbly and dug into him, and it was very hot under the skins. But he was used to being uncomfortable, so he did not really mind. The important thing was to get well away from the village without being found out.

It seemed a long time before he heard the traders coming back, talking among themselves in their strange accent. He felt the cart lift and jolt as they yoked the bullocks to it. There were shouts of goodbye, a few more jolting movements, and the cart moved slowly on its way. Atek hardly dared to breathe. He knew that if he were found before they were clear of the village, his uncle's anger would be terrible and life for him would be even worse than it was now. He must not be found.

CHAPTER THREE

It was a long day. The cart jolted slowly on. Sometimes it stopped for a time – while the traders ate and drank, Atek guessed. He was hungry, but he was used to not eating very much, so he could bear it. He knew it was still far too soon to risk being found out. They were quite near enough to send him back to the village.

He was growing very stiff and longed to stretch his limbs, but did not dare. It grew stiflingly hot too, so that he could hardly breathe.

Evening came, which was a relief because it was much cooler. The cart stopped. The traders were making a camp for themselves. He knew they lit a fire, because he could smell the smoke. There was a lot of talk round the fire, and more eating and drinking, he supposed. Then everything went quiet.

Now was his chance to stretch his legs and find something to eat while the traders slept. He slid backwards, out from under the skins, onto the ground. His legs nearly gave way as he tried to stand, so he did a silent dance until the circulation came back. They had stopped in a large clearing in a wood. Outlined against the remains of the fire, he could see the black shapes of the traders, stretched out in sleep. Nearby, the bullocks were asleep too. They did not seem to have posted any guards, as far as he could see. He counted six shapes – and there had been six traders at the village.

Then another shape, small and black, shot towards him out of the darkness. A furious barking broke out. He had forgotten the dog.

Everyone woke up. Atek started to run, but his legs still felt strange and he didn't get very far. He was dragged to the fire, which they poked into life, so they could see him better. Suspicious eyes looked him over. 'It's the boy from the village,' said a man with a bushy black beard. 'Janaki's nephew.'

A red-haired man shook him. 'What are you doing, boy?' he demanded. 'Did Janaki send you to spy on us?'

'Why should he do that?' one of the other men said. He only had one eye, but he was older than the others and seemed to be in charge. 'Come on, boy, tell us what you're doing!'

'I want to get away,' said Atek. 'And I want to find my father.'

'You can't come with us,' said Bushy Beard. 'Your place is with your uncle.' He looked round at the other traders. 'We should send him back, first thing tomorrow.'

'I'm not going back!'

'You'd not last long out here on your own,' said One-Eye.

'He's not coming with us, that's for sure,' said Red-Hair. 'He'll bring us bad luck, with those eyes.'

'He can't help his eyes,' said One-Eye. Perhaps he understood, Atek thought. 'Would you send him back to Janaki? You know what kind of man he is.'

'That's not our problem,' said Bushy Beard.

'But I think it is, now that he's here. I think we should take a vote on it, but first let's hear his story. What's this about your father, boy?'

So there in the firelight Atek told his story to the traders and they listened with great care. Afterwards, One-Eye said gently, 'I think your aunt was right. Your father's dead. You would have had news of him by now if he were still alive. Would you want to come with us even if you knew you had no hope of finding him?'

'I never want to go back to my uncle. I'd rather come with you and learn to be a trader.'

'Then let's see what we all think.' They took a vote. Two of them – Red-Hair and Bushy Beard – raised their hands to say he should be sent back. The other four voted for him to stay.

'That's it then,' said One-Eye. 'It's decided. You come with us.'

The two men who had been outvoted grumbled among themselves. But the others gave him food and showed him where he could sleep, and when he lay

down the dog curled up beside him. Life was already very much better.

It went on getting better. Atek enjoyed the journey. He did what he could to help, looking for food and firewood, caring for the bullocks. Even the two men who had voted for sending him back soon came to treat him as one of themselves. They gave him a goatskin pouch, such as they all carried, so he had somewhere safe to put his bird whistle, and a leather water bottle. He found himself thinking that he would not mind if the journey never came to an end. Every day there was something new to see. Each evening, as they sat round the camp fire, the men would tell stories – old legends of heroes and gods and demons; tales of their own adventures, of scorching sun and bitter cold, of bandits who tried to rob them, and lost paths, and tricks people had played on them (and usually come to regret). Atek had never been so happy.

After the first few days they came to a desert land of sand and rock and baking heat. 'At the other side we shall reach a small river,' One-Eye explained. 'We shall follow it, and the next and the next, until we come at last to the Great River. On that Great River lies the city of Harappa. That's where we shall exchange our silver.'

The ground here was too soft for the wheels of the cart. Atek helped to take them off and lay them on top of the cart. Then they pulled it along like a sledge. They took it in turns to pull the cart themselves, so as to save the bullocks work. 'There's not enough water for them,' One-Eye said. 'We can't work them again until we reach the far side.' It was fiercely hot, with no shelter at all from the sun. Atek was thirsty all the time, but they only had a few water bottles which they had filled before they crossed the desert. They took it in turns to have sips.

It was a relief when they saw a few low scrubby trees, and more rocks, and then at last a stream running downhill. They camped there for the night, glad to leave the desert behind them. They ate well, drank as much as they wanted, and then settled down to sleep.

It was the dog barking that woke Atek. He sat up. The fire was out, so he couldn't see anything, only the black uneven line of the scrubby trees against the starlit sky. Then he saw that the uneven line was moving, that different shapes were coming their way, shapes that were not trees, shapes like men with sticks. He shouted. The dog went on barking.

He heard someone call, 'Bandits!' He heard thudding sounds, cries, the dog yelping. What should he do? He couldn't fight an enemy he couldn't see.

Nearby was a huge rock. Bent low, he ran to hide behind it. Then he peered round, just enough to make out what was happening, as his eyes grew used to the dark.

By now some of the traders were awake and trying to fight back. But they had been taken by surprise and the bandits had great sticks. Atek saw them rise and fall against the night sky, again and again. There were horrible cries.

Then it was all over. There were only about five people still on their feet. Were they traders, or bandits? They went to the cart and hitched the bullocks to it. Then they began to lead it away.

Atek knew what that meant. The bandits had

won. They were stealing the silver. But what had become of his new friends, the traders?

CHAPTER FOUR

Atek was too scared to move out from the rock until morning came. Then he saw a terrible sight. Everywhere about the ashes of the camp fire the traders lay sprawled on bruised grass. They did not look like men who were sleeping. Atek went to look more closely. Every one of them was dead. Then he found the dog. They had killed it too.

He had been too shocked for tears, but he did cry then, for the dog, for his new friends; and for himself, alone in a strange land.

Then he thought: 'The bandits might come back, now it's daytime, to see if they missed anything. I can't stay here.'

But where should he go? He was quite sure now that his father was dead. He had probably been killed by bandits, just like the traders. But Atek had no intention of going back to the village. He would rather take his chance with bandits and hunger and wild animals than do that.

He wiped his eyes with his cloak, found himself a stout stick, just in case, and set out to follow the flow of the stream. It was the only thing he could possibly do.

He walked all that day, without really thinking about it. Sometimes, if he saw berries that he knew were good to eat, he picked them and put them in his leather pouch. He knew he would have to eat some time, though at the moment he did not feel in the least hungry. He filled his water bottle from the stream, so he would always have something to drink. Otherwise, he just walked until night time. Then he curled up under the lowest shrub he could find and tried to sleep.

As the days passed they all seemed to merge into one. There were differences. Sometimes he saw no one at all. Sometimes he met other travellers, and hid until they were out of sight. Sometimes he found enough to eat. Sometimes it was hard to find anything. After a few days his leather sandals dropped to bits. The stony track cut his feet, but he just kept going. The path alongside the stream went gradually downhill, the stream grew wider. At last it became a river. Now and then he saw a boat, with people rowing. He'd never seen boats before.

Then he came to a place where the river joined a larger one. This must be the second river One-Eye had spoken about. Two more, and he would be at the Great River, and perhaps find the city of Harappa. The thought cheered him for a little while.

But it grew hotter and there were fewer trees and more villages, and he found it harder and harder to keep going. There seemed to be even less to eat. Some days he had nothing at all. Other days he begged food at a village. Sometimes kind people gave him something. More often they shouted, 'Go away, White Eyes!' Once, they set the dogs on him and he had to run for his life.

Then he found he was forgetting where he was or why he was there and where he was going, or even who he was. Now and then, he just fell over, exhausted, and went to sleep where he dropped. Even when he was walking he felt dizzy and strange.

He no longer knew how many rivers he had walked beside. He just kept walking. At least he wasn't hungry any more, just very thirsty. But he knew he would not be able to keep going much longer. He seemed to have no strength in his legs, no energy at all.

'Just one more step!' he kept telling himself.

He was beside a great, wide river, shining in the sun. It shone so brightly it hurt his eyes. He wanted shade, more than anything, but there was no shade. He gave all his attention to putting one foot in front of the other, forcing his legs to go on.

Then he knew he couldn't do it any more. There was one low tree beside the path. He stopped beside it and simply fell down and knew he could not get up again.

After that, many strange things seemed to be going through his head. There was a long time of darkness and nightmares; and voices speaking a long way off. Then there were hands touching him, kind hands. Then he was lifted up, and there was an uncomfortable jolting, with more voices talking away somewhere. Then he was lying down again, on a soft bed that was gently rocking.

From time to time people would come and bathe his forehead or his feet and give him things to drink. Otherwise he was left in peace, which was a relief, because he felt terrible. Horrible nightmares chased through his head. He was aching all over and never seemed able to rest, in spite of the comfortable bed.

Then came a time of deep sleep, from which he woke feeling odd and light and very weak, but much more like himself. A woman sat by the bed, spinning. For a moment he thought it was his aunt. Then he saw that she was not as tall, and her hair was more curly and her face was fatter. The only thing the same was that she looked at him kindly. As soon as she saw he was looking at her, she put down her spindle and came to bring him water to drink.

'Who are you?' he asked her. 'Where am I?'

'I am Wimala, wife of Santi. You have been very ill. You are on our boat.'

He managed to raise himself up enough to look

around. Near his head were two blocks of pale shiny stone. There was an awning overhead, keeping the sun off him. Beyond it, he could see a man working the oars. He was tall and strong. Further off, he could just see the river bank, stretching gently upwards. Everywhere there were small fields, full of growing things.

'Where are you taking me?'

'To our home,' Wimala said. 'To Harappa.'

CHAPTER FIVE

So Atek had, after all, reached Harappa, the city the traders were going to. He had to have help to get off the boat, because his legs were still very wobbly. But he was quite well enough to stare in amazement at the city. He had seen nothing like it before.

Towering over it all was a great citadel, with a wall around it. Atek could not have dreamed that a wall could be so strong and high. Just below the wall stood a massive building – built of brick, like everything else. 'That's the granary,' explained Santi, 'where all our food is stored for the year, from harvest to harvest. It's nearly harvest time now.'

They were walking up the slope through fields full of ripening wheat and barley.

Santi and Wimala were not going towards the citadel, but to a walled town to the east of it, on lower ground – though it was still well above the river level. Atek saw houses, masses of them, built together in straight lines – not just huts, like his uncle's house, but brick houses, many of them two floors high. It must be like an antheap, he thought, with so many people living there that you could never hope to count them.

There were a lot of people outside the town too, loading or unloading boats with goods – Santi's was far from being the only boat on the river – or driving bullock carts up to the citadel or the town. There were groups of traders, too, like Atek's lost friends, returning safely from a long journey or setting out on a new one. It was exciting and strange and different and made Atek feel much better.

They made their way first along a wide street that was so crowded with people and carts that it was hard to get through the crush. In one place, two bullock carts had blocked the way and a fierce argument was going on between the drivers, while behind them in either direction more carts were coming to a halt, while angry drivers shouted for the way to be cleared. Just beyond the traffic jam, they saw two important-looking men pushing through the crowd. 'They'll be going to sort it out,' Santi explained.

Atek was so busy watching what was going on that he tripped on a stone slab in the middle of the road. Santi grabbed his arm to steady him. 'You have to watch out for the drain covers,' he said. Then he explained how all the waste from the houses ran into drainage channels in the streets, which were covered over with brick or stone. 'It makes our houses much pleasanter,' he said. Atek thought that was probably true, though it also made the streets rather smelly.

Then Santi and Wimala turned into a narrow street, with tall houses on either side, and another and another. On the corner of the very next street Santi said, 'Here we are. This is our house.'

They went through a high doorway into a passage. 'That's the bathroom, there on the left,'

Santi said, pointing to a small room with a brick floor. 'The latrine's next to it.' He had to explain what a latrine was for. Atek was used to using anywhere outside.

They turned a corner, past a little shrine with a bronze statue of the Mother Goddess, and on into an open courtyard. In one corner an old woman was cooking over a fire. Beside her a little girl was playing with a toy cart, a tiny version of the bullock carts in the street outside. 'This is my mother, Padmi, and our daughter, Tara.' Santi explained to the old woman how Atek came to be there.

Padmi smiled at Atek. 'Supper will soon be ready. First you must wash and rest.'

Santi led Atek up a staircase to the room above. 'You can sleep here, or up on the roof if it's very hot.' Then he laid a hand on the boy's shoulder. 'Now I must go and get the stone brought up from the boat. That was the purpose of our journey, after all.' He smiled. 'But it seems the Goddess knew there was another purpose – to find you. Be sure that this is now your home for as long as you need to stay.'

It took no time at all for Atek to feel at home.

He learned that Santi was a cutter of seals – like the ones that had been used to mark the packages that the traders had brought to the village. The seals were made from a stone called steatite. 'Everything that is sent out of the town must be sealed, and every merchant has his own seal,' Santi explained. 'So this is important work. If you wish, I can teach you how to do it.'

Atek had told Santi and Wimala about his father, and they too had agreed that Romesh must be dead. He had put away his hopes of finding his father. Now he was being offered a chance to start a new life with kind people.

So by day he worked on the seals. Santi was a good teacher, but it was difficult work. First Atek learned how to cut square shapes from the blocks of steatite, like the two Santi had brought on his boat. That was the easy bit. After that, patterns had to be cut into the squares. 'You see,' explained Santi, 'everything has to be carved so that when the seal is pressed on the clay it makes a raised pattern. So it's important that you can see what the pattern is. You must carve it with the utmost care.'

At first, Atek made a horrible mess of the work. He tried to carve bullocks and tigers and trees, and they all looked the same – like shapeless splodges. As for the lettering, that was harder still. First he had to learn what the strange lines meant, and that took a long time as well. Carving them on the small squares of steatite was very difficult indeed. But gradually it became easier.

'You have skilled hands,' Santi said approvingly one day. He was looking at a seal Atek had just finished, with a hump-backed bull on it. 'You've learned very quickly. This is good work.'

In the evenings the family would all eat together. There was always plenty to eat. Afterwards, they sat around and told stories. Sometimes the neighbours would join them too. At these times Tara would climb onto Atek's knee. 'She likes you,' Wimala said, and it was true. Tara followed him everywhere she could. Atek liked her too. She was a happy child.

Best of all was that no one in Harappa had ever made any comment about Atek's eyes. There were so many people in the city, coming and going from far and near, that no one seemed to think there was anything strange about Atek. They treated him like any other human being. He felt as if he really belonged, for the first time in his life.

Soon after he came to the city the crops in the fields were cut and stored in the granary. And then the floods came. Atek watched from the safety of the town as the river rose and rose, day after day. Rain came too, and water rushed all day along the drains in the streets. Before long the river spread right up to the edge of the city. It looked as if at any moment it might come into the houses. 'Why isn't anyone afraid?' he asked Santi as they stood one day watching the water coming closer to the city.

'Because it happens every year. The flood is dangerous if you don't take care, but it also brings us life. When it goes down in the autumn it leaves the fields covered with a layer of mud called silt. That makes a rich soil for the crops, so they grow well and we never go hungry.'

Atek lived with Santi and his family through two floods. At the end of the second flood, Santi said to him, 'You've learned all you can from me. Now, I'm going to send you on a long journey to learn more. There's a skilled seal cutter in another great city called Mohenjo Daro. I want you to go and stay with him for three months, to learn all you can. Then, when you come back, you will be ready to set up as a seal maker in your own right.'

Atek felt honoured, but also afraid. He didn't want to leave this place where he was so happy, even for a short time. But he knew Santi wanted the best for him, so he agreed.

He set out again on his travels. This time he went by boat with other men who were going south, and took many things with him – some seals he had made, to show what he could do, a change of clothes, a set of tools for making seals. He also took the pouch the traders had given him, and in it the whistle his father had made. He felt as if it brought him luck.

Tara cried when he left. He hugged her. 'I'll bring you a present when I come back,' he promised.

CHAPTER SIX

Atek quickly felt at home in Mohenjo Daro. The city was so like Harappa, in its buildings and its streets and its drains and everything else, that it was easy to forget he was a long way from Santi and his family. He missed them, but he enjoyed meeting new people and learning new things.

Trita, the seal cutter he was staying with, had no family. He was old and sometimes bad tempered. But he welcomed Atek and praised his skill. 'You've been well taught,' he said. 'But the best seal cutters are born, not made. I know you're going to be one of them. Just like me and Santi.'

When the three months were nearly over, Atek began to plan his journey home. But first, there was one thing he had to do in Mohenjo Daro. 'I need to find a present to take to Tara,' he told Trita. 'Do you know who's the best toymaker in the city?'

Trita grunted. 'I don't have much to do with toys. But I know who they say is best. He lives near Nandi the potter's shop. I forget his name. Ask for the cripple with white eyes.'

'White eyes?' said Atek. 'Like me?' His heart was thudding and his voice sounded strange.

Trita looked at him in surprise. Then he shrugged. 'I suppose so. I've never really thought about it. The world's a big place. You get all sorts.'

Atek set out to find the toymaker's shop. It took him a long time, and much asking for directions. But at last he found himself outside the one-storey house where the toymaker lived. He took a deep breath and stepped inside, wondering what he would find.

There were toys everywhere, on shelves, on the floor. There were animals with heads you could move up and down, and carts and rattles – and whistles, made of clay, not wood. But there was no

54

one in the room. Atek saw a door leading to a courtyard. There, he found a man crouched by a fire, cooking something. He had his back to Atek. He had black, curly hair and broad shoulders and looked no different from anybody else.

Atek coughed, loudly. The man stood up slowly, with the help of a stick, and Atek saw that he only had one leg.

Then he turned round. Even though Atek had expected it, the man's eyes were still a shock. They weren't white at all, but a clear grey colour, like water on a dull day. They looked at him, steadily, but with a question too.

'I'm told you make the best toys,' Atek said. 'I want a present for a little girl.'

The man smiled. 'Come with me.' He hobbled into the shop and sat down on a stool. 'Is there anything you like here?'

'Lots of things,' said Atek. But he wasn't looking at the toys. He couldn't stop watching the man. Did his own eyes look like the toymaker's? Was it something like this his aunt had meant, when she'd told him his eyes weren't white at all? It was good to think that he wasn't alone, that there was someone else with the same unusual eyes. They were strange, but not terrible or frightening.

Atek realised that the toymaker was waiting for him to choose a toy. He was beginning to look impatient. Suddenly – he didn't quite know why – Atek reached into his pouch and took out the bird whistle. He passed it to the toymaker. 'Could you make something like this?'

The man took it. Then he went very still. He stared at the small, wooden thing in his hand. Atek was beginning to wonder if he would ever speak again, when he asked, 'Where did you get this?' His voice sounded husky.

'My father made it for me, before he went away.'

The toymaker stared and stared, at the toy bird, at Atek, and back again. The room seemed to have gone very still. Atek felt odd, afraid, yet as if something very important was about to happen.

'Who was your father?' asked the toymaker at last.

'Romesh, son of Atek. That's why I'm called Atek, after my grandfather.'

Atek had never seen so many different expressions pass over one face in such a short time. 'So you are Atek,' said the man, as if he needed to be very sure.

Atek nodded. He could hardly breathe, his heart was thudding so fast. The man was still holding the whistle in his open palm, though his eyes never left Atek. 'I think you must be my son,' he said at last. His tone was full of wonder, as if he could not quite believe it.

Atek could not believe it either. He had been so sure that his father was dead. How could this man be his father, this crippled toymaker in the city far away from the village of his birth? Atek had never heard that his father had only one leg, and if he had he would surely not have been able to travel so far from home.

'If you're my father,' he asked, 'why did you go away – and how did you do it? And why did you never come back?'

The man pointed to his leg. 'I've not always been like this. I had an accident, here in the city. I was knocked down by a bullock cart – someone frightened the animals and they bolted. After that, I could never walk far. I knew then I would never go home. But I sent word with the traders, more than once. Did you not hear?'

Atek shook his head. 'We never knew what had happened. We thought you were dead.' He knew then that he did believe it – this was his father. But why didn't he feel more pleased?

'Is your mother here with you?'

'She died, a long time ago.'

Romesh bent his head. Atek wondered what he was thinking. After a moment his father looked up again. Atek saw there were tears in his eyes. 'There's a meal ready. Eat with me and you can tell me all that has happened.'

Atek hardly noticed what the food was. Neither of them ate very much. Instead, they talked and talked, about all that had happened since they last saw each other. Romesh listened gravely to what Atek told him about the way his uncle had treated him. 'I never trusted Janaki. I didn't want Kamala to marry him. But I didn't think things would get so bad.'

'Why did you go away?' asked Atek, again.

'I thought I might find somewhere better to live. Then I meant to come back for you and your mother. But it all went wrong. I should never have left, I can see that now.'

'I don't know,' said Atek, slowly. 'Perhaps it was for the best.' Then he got up from where he'd been sitting cross-legged on the floor and went to Romesh and hugged him, and his father hugged him back.

CHAPTER SEVEN

Atek did not want to risk losing his father again. Yet he did not want to stay in Mohenjo Daro. He was part of Santi's family now and he wanted to go back to them. He told Romesh how he felt.

'Then let me come with you to Harappa, on a visit,' suggested Romesh, 'if you think you can cope with a one-legged companion on your journey. I'd like to meet Santi and Wimala. And perhaps I'll find there's room for another toymaker in the city.'

So Romesh went back with Atek to Harappa, taking with him a bag full of toys he had made. When they reached the city, he went to the lodgings reserved for visiting merchants.

'I'll come and meet Santi when you've told them all about me,' he said.

It was strange going back. Atek knew them all so well, and they hadn't changed a bit. Yet he felt different, full of the great news he had to tell them. He walked into the courtyard where they were all sitting down to a meal. Before they had even come to hug him he said, 'I've found my father.'

After that, things happened very quickly. Santi went at once to invite Romesh to come and eat with them. Romesh brought his bag of toys, and gave most of them to Tara. Atek was overjoyed to see how well his father got on with them all.

The next thing he knew, it was all arranged: Romesh would stay in Harappa and find a house where he could set up a toy shop.

'Then you'll have two homes,' said Santi to Atek. 'Two homes, but one family – all of us.'

Atek looked round the courtyard, at Santi and Wimala, who had given him a home and a new life; at old Padmi, and Tara laughing at all the toys – and at his father Romesh, whom he had found just when he had given up all hope. His family, he thought, all of them together. The whistle had indeed brought him luck.